# A Battleaxe and a Metal Arm 14:

## *Test of Faith*

Samuel Fleming

ISBN-13: 978-1-954679-39-9 (paperback)
ISBN-13: 978-1-954679-38-2 (ebook)

Thank you to my Beta Readers

and to my First Reader,

Mel.

# Contents

"We do not suffer one death,
but a thousand smaller ones.
Each pain and loss is a black
rose we must bear."
—undefined

# Previously...

The heroes' journey took them back to the second realm they set foot in—the abandoned barracks ruled over by the giant wizard, Zhug, and his goblin army. Where first they were attacked on sight, this time they were escorted through the hallways as tentative allies. The outcast goblin, Widewill, had been forgiven by Zhug and brought back into the fold of the goblins again.

Stizzai, the goblin leader, and Zhug's obsidian metal men led the heroes through the halls, past the trapdoor to the crypt where the Many-Handed Horror, Shomosk lay in darkness. They led the heroes all the way to Zhug's trophy room and throne, where the giant waited for them. Helesys and Taunauk regaled the wizard with their travels and all that they had learned.

Of all the secrets the heroes had uncovered, Zhug was surprised only by the Voice—that it was the source of their power to bring treasures back after death.

Zhug gave them a giant metal diving crab so that they could journey to the bottom of the endless sea and find the resting place of the Machine of Antrikaumora. He taught Helesys the words to command it, and the words to change the size of the crab, should they need to.

Zhug's kindness did not extend further, however, and the wizard sent them on their way. Through a seam hidden in the treasure room.

Once on the shore of the endless sea, they climbed into the metal crab and began the slow trek beneath the waves. In spite of Taunauk's dislike of water, they descended into the murky depths without issue. Coral and life gave way to a barren ocean and quiet. Soon, not even light from above reached them.

As they passed the time, Taunauk confessed that not all spirits within him were Endroggen—three were different. This gave fuel to Helesys's desire to learn Endroggen rage, and Taunauk's acceptance to teach her.

Her first lesson was that even with her soldier's training, Helesys was always in control of her actions in battle. In those times she felt like a weapon, absent thought and fear—she was not the weapon.

Soon they passed dark metal spires, like a jagged city rising from the depths. As the spires grew more numerous, the pressure of the deep abated. But before they could reach safety, they were set upon by a kraken, and desperately evaded its grasp. Helesys called upon her wand and the Gar of Shéslang, and was able to pause the creature with her holding spell for just long enough to get past it.

Moments later, they crashed onto a dry, silty floor and found the outside completely dry and cold. From there they walked across the sea floor, set upon on all sides by the growing spires. The entire city was a rune, special spells writ large to keep the crushing ocean at bay. And though most of their walk was peaceful, the heroes suspected a trap was coming.

Eventually, they happened upon a swarm of eels—the same horrid creatures that had attacked at night aboard the Malorienta. Together, they bested them with walls of ice, arcane blasts, and Endroggen rage.

Soon they came to a mound of metal. They descended down the strange stairs. Runes of containment covered the surface and were writ large through the twisting passages—measures to contain the power of the Machine and to prevent rebirth.

They pressed forward in spite of the danger and in spite of lingering deaths. In the halls they were set upon by twisted marionettes made of ironwood, impervious to normal magic and weapons. A vicious battle ensued, and it wasn't until Helesys cut the strings of one puppet that their weakness was found and the group overcome.

Even more troubling as they pressed deeper into the passages was that the heroes's connection to their magic and to their ancestors was growing tenuous. Helesys's wand spoke to her, rather than giving her direction.

They passed through a maze of spikes before coming to a dangerous passage, one marked by Sinatin Koh—suspected to be the name of the infamous Voice at Meridian. The final hallway to the center was wrought with rotating clockwork gears. It was in this final sphere that Helesys found the Machine of Antrikaumora and claimed it as her own.

Helesys seized the Machine—the tiny cube that held such power—and realized the truth of its power: That it was an antimagic generator.

But as she took it, the facility lost its power and was no longer able to contain the oppressing ocean above it. Water began to violently flood the passageways, and Helesys and Taunauk were forced to flee to a random realm—anywhere but beneath the sea.

~ ~ ~

# *The Barren Plains*

Helesys and Taunauk walked across the barren plains, feet falling steady on the cracked ground. A pitiful red sun hung just below the horizon, casting the realm in a blood-red glow.

The last thing they had seen was a great beam of yellow light rising up from the horizon—the same heading that Helesys's wand now directed them to go.

At first, it seemed as if they were alone for a dozen miles in every direction. But in the distance to their right, they heard a commotion—the sound of shifting earth and battle. Across the plains, Terrans rose from under the ground. From so far away, they looked like little more than a distant forest. One that stretched from nearly one horizon to the next.

Instinctively, Helesys kindled power and felt the arcane energy churn in her gauntlet. She felt ready for whatever came their direction.

But nothing did. Groans carried over the landscape, and the grisly crowd began to move and sway.

And somewhere in the mass there was a tiny intermittent blur of movement.

Helesys and Taunauk watched for a minute, before they caught sight of an enormous shadow moving over the landscape—so large and so fast that at first Helesys thought the sun was setting.

It was an enormous bird of prey, soaring across the landscape. In moments, it was upon the group, diving down, and scooping up swathes of creatures in each set of claws. Helesys was spellbound at the sight. Each time she thought she had seen the limits of the creatures in the dungeon, she was proven wrong. The condor across the plains was bigger than the hydra, bigger than the kraken—it might have even been big enough to pluck the Idnauthi ship from the sky.

It swooped back and forth over the mass, cutting swathes through them.

Again, Helesys saw the blur of motion, this time moving away from the herd of creatures. Moving in the same direction as Helesys and Taunauk were.

"Do you think…" Helesys muttered. "Should I signal him?"

"Yes," Taunauk replied. "I think it's him."

She watched the tiny, lone figure until the condor flew off across the horizon. Then she held up her gauntlet and called forth her warding light.

After a tentative breath, the figure started sprinting toward them. Helesys didn't relax her breath until it was close and she saw the rogue's familiar face.

"Well, well, well," Shawn said when he was close. "Could've used you two back there." He was smiling, but his leathers were coated in thin streaks of red, a testament to his battle.

Helesys replied, "You looked like you had everything under control."

Both Helesys and Taunauk returned his smile.

~

The three comrades walked across the barren plains, heading toward the last sighting of the beam of light.

Helesys told him about their journey below the endless sea in the metal crab, and then about the kraken, the eels, and the strange facility that housed the Machine of Antrikaumora.

"You found it?" Shawn asked.

Helesys nodded, then pulled the tiny metal cube from her pocket.

"What does it do?" he asked.

"It makes an antimagic field—"

Shawn startled and practically jumped back from it.

Helesys said, "It's not activated."

Shawn breathed a sigh of relief and relaxed. Meanwhile, Taunauk chuckled.

The rogue eyed him sideways. "it's not funny. Some of us are more *magical* than others." Shawn tentatively grasped the cube and turned it over in his hands. "An awful lot of fuss for something so small," he added, and handed it back to her.

Helesys replied, "Well, this small cube also powered the facility. When I took it the ocean came crashing down on us. We barely made it out before the place flooded." She stuffed the cube back in her pocket and asked, "What happened to you while you were gone? Did you find some more terrible lizards?"

Shawn smirked, but the emotion was fleeting.

When he didn't respond, Helesys pointed to his arms. "I see you found your wrappings again."

"Oh, these? They followed me. They were with me when I made it back to the beach." Shawn slowed and added, "I spoke to the Voice again."

Helesys and Taunauk stopped.

Taunauk asked, "What did it say?"

Shawn said, "Remember how there's been other Chosen, but obviously they failed? The Voice told me why. It said that only a god can kill another god. The other Chosen failed because the wrong one took the shot. When the time comes, when we've got him beaten—it has to be me that does it."

There was something else in Shawn's voice, though; a weariness that dragged down his usual mirth.

Helesys asked, "There's something else, isn't there? What else did you speak about with the Voice?"

Shawn shrugged. "Most of it was about myself, actually. It was beautiful to fly. I'm not even sure there's a word that could do it justice. *Breathtaking*, maybe? I even flew across the realms.

"But when I landed on that beach and I wrapped my arms again—became Terran again—it was… It felt right, I guess. Somehow, being Terran and feeling the sun on my face was even more beautiful than flying. I just can't reconcile giving up the life of a god *and* the life of a Terran. Where do I go from there?"

As silence fell, Taunauk placed a hand on the rogue's shoulder. "No one can answer the question of *who you are*, except for you. And while you dwell on it, find solace in the present task and this moment."

Shawn nodded and smiled painfully. "Remind me again how you got so wise."

Taunauk shrugged. "I spent much of my youth training with the elders and listening to them. They were keen to pass along their wisdom."

"That sounds an awful lot like you got stuck listening to monologues."

"More or less," Taunauk replied, then patted him on the shoulder.

Shawn added, "Let me guess: *To task*." Shawn lowered his voice comically.

Helesys jested, "Next time say it deeper."

The three continued on in the perpetual red twilight, sharing laughter between them.

Though they were plagued by questions and by the looming confrontation with the Wolf King, Helesys pushed those concerns aside. For those miles across the barren plains, she strove to follow the advice of her friend.

~

They walked for hours, though in the perpetual sunset they had no idea of knowing just how long had passed.

Twice, zombies rose from the ground. The first group were Terran, a shambling, sprawling mass of hundreds—nothing compared to the group that had surrounded Shawn upon his first arrival. The three heroes tore through the undead horde like sickles through wheat. Shawn became a blur, while Taunauk and his Endroggen spirits sprawled out across the field.

Meanwhile, Helesys called on her arcane blasts and spear. She reached for her memories of her mother and her sister, and tried to harness the power of rage.

But each time she thought of something other than battle— each time she thought of anything at all—it felt as if her blasts flew errantly, and her spear didn't quite strike true. Truth be it that the zombies were so numerous that even an errant blast killed something, and they were so weak that even a mistimed strike broke them in two, but Helesys noticed.

She knew there was power in Endroggen rage, yet for her it seemed merely a distraction. The weaver grew frustrated with herself. So much else came easily: Spells came to memory when they were needed, fighting maneuvers too. But Endroggen blood magic eluded her during that battle.

When zombies appeared the second time, the mottled, rotting flesh was the only thing that was similar. Their shapes were strange. The Terrans that rose were misshapen or asymmetrical—one arm longer than the rest, hands as big as torsos, or uneven legs that gave them a horrific, galloping gait, and those were the least strange. Others had wings, the skin long since sloughed off so that they looked like long, gnarled fingers. Others were gargantuan, four-legged beasts that had never been Terran, but were far too decomposed to tell what they might've been before. They crawled from the ground and lumbered on ragged limbs, some without even muscle or ligaments to move them—

Helesys churned power and thought of the bonemen from the cannibals' realm. Foul magic steeped this desert.

But not even those beasts would deny them passage. Taunauk's axe cleaved creatures in two, while Shawn's blades severed limbs and heads. Helesys's blasts tore holes clean through the largest creatures and they fell like great trees amongst the smaller fodder.

As each creature fell, it vanished—reborn elsewhere in the realms.

When Helesys was breathing hard from exertion and her gauntlet felt half-numb from use, the last of the beasts was gone. The group could rest, but instead they pushed onward across the desert, driven by powers and pressures they had just begun to understand.

~ ~ ~

# City of Iron and Dust

Spires rose in the distance, like a graveyard of swords sticking up out of the ground—a city rising out of the dust. For a moment, Helesys was taken back beneath the endless sea, to the dark metal spires that rose from the abyss.

But as they grew near the iron walls, Helesys saw that this was only a pale imitation of the underwater prison of the Machine. The spires underwater had been impossibly tall, their arrangement sprawling—so large that Helesys and Taunauk had only traversed to the center because they walked directly through it.

The city in front of them, though immense, was finite. Its walls did not stretch out to the horizon, nor did its spires scrape the sky.

"What's wrong?" Shawn asked.

His voice brought Helesys out of her trance—she'd stopped on the cracked dunes and stared at the city.

The elf shook her head. "The city… It reminds me of the place where we found the Machine of Antrikaumora. Even the magic feels similar."

Taunauk asked, "Are you sure about this place?"

She nodded. "The seam is in there. I can feel it."

Shawn sighed. "What should we do, go up and knock on the front gate?"

Taunauk shrugged. "Unless you'd rather fly over the walls."

The rogue shook his head. "I've had enough flying to last me a while. I rather like keeping my feet on the ground."

The heroes walked the last half mile to the city wall. The rusty iron rose some five stories high and the seamless face of it stretched out miles to either side.

Shawn groaned. "It's going to take us forever to find the gate."

Helesys eyed the bottom of the structure. In some place the iron walls continued into the rusty-colored earth, but in other places they stopped short. In those places, there was different rock between the cracked ground and the iron wall—striped and porous.

Helesys stooped closer to investigate. Taunauk followed.

'What do you make of that?" she asked.

"It is different," the Endroggen grumbled.

"Clearly," Shawn jested from behind them.

Taunauk shook his head. "Too different. It is not from this realm. Look." He pointed down the length of the wall, and Helesys saw the same striped pattern of alien rock continuing into the distance. "It runs throughout the length of the city."

Shawn asked, "What does that mean?"

Helesys said, "The city is from a different realm."

~

It was some hours longer walking around the wall of the city before they found a gate. It was made of intricate curling bars of iron, and Shawn shivered at the towering thing.

"What is it about iron that pains you?" Helesys asked.

Shawn pulled his hood back and pondered the gates a moment. Then he shrugged. "I'm not sure. Why are werewolves afraid of silver?"

*Silver has antibacterial properties*, her wand whispered, *and it impedes the healing of some monstrous creatures like vampyres and werewolves.*

Helesys smirked and repeated this aloud for the rogue.

"Huh. Well, what does your wand say about wrought iron?" he asked.

Helesys heard her wand and replied, "It says that silver's properties are common knowledge."

Shawn let out a mocking laugh. "So I'm special."

Taunauk grumbled, "Don't let it go to your head."

As the three approached, there were calls from the gates telling them to halt. The heroes stopped some yards from the entrance and watched the commotion behind the iron bars.

A small section of the bars began to warp and twist, glowing a dull red and causing the surrounding air to shimmer. Two elves stepped forward in full armor, ribbons and regalia hung from their chests. Of these, Helesys's eyes were drawn to only one emblem—a single wolf's head, engraved prominently on their shoulder pauldrons.

The taller and more weathered of the two elves addressed them. His eyes were sharp and his voice firm with rank and command.

"Ho! Who has crossed the weathered sea?" he said.

Helesys answered, "We are Helesys Byyra, Taunauk Aonar, and Soldei Milent. We have fought across the desert and seek passage through the realm."

The younger elf stood fast, hand on the pommel of his sword, and at Helesys's words, he glanced to the commander. His eyes wavered with question, but he didn't speak.

"You're a weaver, then?" the commander asked. "You seek a seam to travel by?"

Helesys nodded.

The commander's eyes drifted to each of the heroes in turn. Helesys watched his face soften and grow weary. He was old for an elf, and it was written plain about him.

"It will take time," he said finally. "The cabal will want to meet with you before they grant you access. They are amenable, but they have… protocols. If you do not mind a day's respite, you can likely be on your way without conflict."

Taunauk and Shawn looked to her expectantly. The rogue shrugged.

"Doesn't look like we have much choice," Shawn replied.

Helesys tried to keep an even tone. "We have traveled far and have much farther to go. So long as the cabal is as amenable as you say, we agree."

The commander nodded and beckoned them to follow through the twisted bars. Once they stepped inside, the iron glowed and twisted closed behind them.

~

On the other side of the wrought-iron gate, towers of iron stretched up above them, the gaps filled with squat buildings of sandstone bricks. The towers of which were few compared to the other buildings. Faces peered out from the doorways and windows of these first buildings—Terrans that heard the shifting gates and entry of newcomers. They peered curiously at the heroes.

"Welcome to Civirrea," the commander said. "The city of iron and dust."

"Fitting name," Shawn muttered.

Though the streets were clear, they were still the same cracked earth as outside the walls. Sand and scraps of cloth blew through the streets. Whatever had been of the city, the desert had taken it over. The buildings were lined with scrawling letters—Helesys eyed these as they walked. No magic came from them, but the script felt familiar to Helesys.

It wasn't until they were several blocks inside that they saw other Terrans out on the streets. Humans and elves worked beside one another in booths cut into the sides of the sandstone buildings, hawking cloth and clay sculptures. Helesys watched a moment at one such booth as a wrinkled woman looked closely at green beads for her already adorned hair. She paid for them with stones, counting them out with a shaky hand. It was the first mix of currency that Helesys could recall. It was a moment before she shook of the strangeness of the sight.

Helesys smiled and stepped hurriedly to catch up with the others. It was the first time they had seen such trade in the realms, and questions were already forming in her mind. She resolved to wait, and watch as they crossed the next several blocks to the tower in the center of the city.

~

Inside, the tower was brighter than Helesys expected. The outside had seemed a dull gray, a color that reflected shadow instead of light. But inside, the walls were polished so that as one's gaze rose from the floor to ceiling; the sheen grew progressively brighter. Light seemed to filter in from the doorways and also from holes in the inner walls.

Helesys's eyes drifted to the furnishings. A long bar ran the length of the side wall, and several small tables and benches littered the room. Upon closer inspection, she realized that each was not just the same metal as the walls, but seamlessly jutting out from the metal—as if the tower and its furnishings had been forged from the same single mass.

Shawn sat at the nearest side bench and sighed. Helesys and Taunauk remained standing.

"My name is Chetan Thistlelin," the commander said. He removed his helmet and set it on the bar with a clang. Then he sat and gestured absently at his companion. "And this is Japag."

The other soldier nodded curtly and stood beside him.

Two other soldiers entered, and Chetan addressed them. "Inform Elder Lorainne that these travelers seek an audience with her and the cabal. And bring a tankard of water for our guests." They departed as quickly as they arrived.

Chetan turned to the heroes, hands clasped in front of him. "You have questions. Everyone has questions."

Helesys had been about to ask, but Shawn blurted out, "What in the spirits is this place?"

Chetan smirked. "This is Civirrea. It's one of the oldest remaining places in the realms, or so the sorcerers say—I'm not *that* old."

Helesys asked, "The metal spires and the stone buildings aren't from the same place?"

The commander shook his head. "I've seen some of the sandstone dwellings carved out in my time. The spires are far older."

"Stranger, too," Taunauk added. The barbarian curiously eyed the smooth lines of the walls and passages.

Chetan said, "Isn't that always the way with the past? The old ways seem strange or barbaric. They are merely different."

Helesys replied, "Spoken with the reverence of an elf."

He nodded. "Indeed, but my sentiment comes from having lived much longer in here in the realms than outside."

"In the city of Novissimé, you mean."

Chetan's brow wrinkled in confusion. "I don't know a city by that name."

Helesys said, "I am still remembering, but there was an elven city named Novissimé—to hear it told it was the *only* elven city. I still don't remember what year this was."

Chetan sat back in his chair, suppressing a look of defeat. "Where is this city?"

"In the mountains. I don't yet remember the name of the range or the country."

After a long moment, he replied, "That doesn't bode well for our people. In my time we were many. We were spread across the twin continents. In that life, I was a smith." He grimaced. "Your other questions will have to wait for the cabal, I think. For now, you will have food and water, then you may walk the streets immediately surrounding the spire with an escort. I will send for you when I hear word from the sorcerers."

The commander left suddenly, waving in another soldier to accompany them and Japag.

Helesys's gaze lingered on the bar after he left. She had so very many questions, and so few Terrans that she could ask.

~

Helesys, Taunauk, and Shawn were given water and rice cakes. Then they walked the streets of Civirrea while the city moved around them. They were just outside a main thoroughfare and Helesys found herself walking toward the bustle of the nearby street. In the distance, there was a steady stream of people compared to the trickles they had seen so far.

It was the first time Helesys could remember walking without purpose. It felt strange—inconceivable, even—and she had to force herself to walk slowly.

She forced herself to stop at a nearby booth that was cut into the sandstone. Two human women wrapped in light dresses worked a bellows and a kiln. Heat wafted through the opening, earthen and salty, and Helesys felt a pang of respect to work in such heat.

"Be with you in a moment," the woman in purple called as she pumped the bellows.

The weaver's eyes fell to the intricate trinkets on the shelves. Stone animals, pottery, and combs. She lingered there, looking at one marble-white comb.

Helesys meant to call back, that she and the others were merely looking, but Shawn interrupted her.

"Where do you think they get it all from?" he asked.

The woman came to the front, wiping her hands and then the sweat from her brow. "Like anything?"

Again, Helesys's eyes fell to the comb. The shopkeep smiled and plucked it from the shelf. "A fitting color for a princess. It matches your hair."

"Pardon?" Helesys said.

"Every pretty lady should have an equally beautiful comb." She set it on the counter between them. "What have you got?

Come back with anything good from the mines? Stone, bone, jewels…"

Helesys snapped out of her trance. For a moment, she thought this human knew her or her family, but it had been a silly thought. Clearly, she assumed Helesys and the others were just other workers from the city.

She pulled her pack around and scrounged through it, realization dawning on her that she had little that was worth—just her weapons and magic items—and none of those she was willing to part with.

Shawn dropped a dark blue stone on the counter, this size of a thumbnail. "Will that cover it?"

A smile flitted across the shopkeep's eyes. "You've got a deal," she replied, trying to keep the excitement from her face. "The comb is yours, miss. You're a lucky girl." She turned and walked back to the kiln.

Helesys carefully picked up the comb, as if it were poisonous instead of beautiful. "You didn't have to do that," she said, not looking at Shawn.

Shawn plucked the comb from her hands. "I didn't do it for you." He ran it through his thin hair and smirked before handing it back to her. "That's the first non-weapon I've seen you look at like that."

Helesys took it with a smile, then ran it through her own white hair, snagging twice. Every new realm they went to, the illusion of long hair returned. Helesys let it go, and found the comb ran through her shoulder-length hair easily. Afterward, she stowed it in her pack.

Shawn had already turned to walk toward the main street.

"Thanks," Helesys said.

Shawn turned over his shoulder and smiled. "Don't mention it." The rogue looked surprised toward Taunauk—the barbarian was staring at him intently, eyes narrowed. "Did you want one too, big guy?"

"Yes."

"Oh, but, uh…" Shawn stammered. He looked as if he was going to point to Taunauk's shaved head and face, then thought better. He turned to walk back to the counter, but Taunauk strode forward and clasped his shoulder.

"I jest," the Endroggen said heartily. "Come, maybe they have furs or another lemur for you to ride on."

Helesys shook her head and smiled, then followed behind her comrades.

~

Here the city seemed to open up so that Helesys could see the red sky above, the iron spires reaching toward it like the fingers of a colossal armored hand. The smell of kiln fire mixed with spices, smells appearing and disappearing quickly on the dry wind. The people were a mix, too. Most were clad in long bright robes, but a few wore armor and Helesys saw several more gathered around a weaponsmith's booth.

Though they were in an unfamiliar place, she felt tension lift from her shoulders as they passed into the main street crowd. In spite of the heroes' armored appearance, no one on the street seemed curious of them. Even the guards or soldiers paid them no mind—each Terran busy with their own business. Helesys found it both pleasant and dumbfounding not to be the center of concern.

So she merely walked with her comrades, taking in the sights and sounds. Even Shawn was silent with observation. Helesys even briefly forgot about the Japag and the other soldiers following a considerate distance behind them.

They stopped at stalls of woven fabric, others of pottery, armor, and weapons. Helesys and Shawn took in the sights, while Taunauk seemed content to follow and to speak silently with his elders.

It was some time before Japag addressed them and led them back to the iron spire. The sorcerers' cabal was ready to meet with them.

~ ~ ~

# The Iron Spire

They walked back into the iron spire and up a spiral staircase in its heart. Helesys felt the light touch of claustrophobia as they ascended and the walls tightened around them. They passed dozens of landings, and down some of the halls, Helesys saw soldiers conversing.

Some uncountable floors later, Japag led them down a corridor to a wide room. The whole of it was arranged as a meeting area—crude metal chairs rose up from the floor in a circular pattern. The far wall was cut away and overlooked the city. Three elves in white robes stood at the window and turned to greet them. They each wore a necklace adorned with a wolf's head.

The man in the center spoke first. "Thank you, Japag. That will be all for now. Please wait outside." He brought a withered hand to his chest and touched his necklace. Japag returned the gesture before stepping outside.

The woman on the right said the old words, "*Diuturno silentium.*" Though Shawn flinched slightly, Helesys recognized it as a warding spell. She felt the aura extend to the doorway, hiding their conversation from traveling outside the room. Taunauk was unmoved, as was the elven man on the left.

Helesys opened herself to any feeling of magic and found that all three elves in front of her were mages.

The center mage smiled warmly, his face creasing in thin lines of age. He was likely very old for an elf and ancient for a human.

"Welcome to Civirrea," he said. He introduced himself as Zinric Uthir. The elven woman was Enhana Deimosh, and the younger man to his left was Sardan Nenkind. "Sit, sit. I trust you've looked around our streets, basked in our civilization? Is it not the envy of the realms?"

The three heroes sat and shared a glance, and it was Helesys that answered.

"It is much more than we expected, and certainly the most like civilization that we've found."

"Vindication!" he gasped. "That is very good. We were ordained as a pillar of hope, and it's good to see that we still are. Of course, warriors such as yourself aren't beholden to stay here. You must be young—few in deaths."

Shawn muttered, "You could say that."

Again, the elder mage smiled. "*Chosen* too."

After a moment of surprise, Helesys asked, "How did you know?"

"I'm old enough to have seen two other groups of chosen," he replied. "There's a confidence about Chosen ones. Others stumble into our city, especially those who have well-suffered through the realms, and they are ready to settle down. Only a few push on—usually the young ones. As I said, there's a look of confidence about the Chosen. Sometimes it's quiet, sometimes it's boisterous. But they are always certain that they're not going to stop here. They are going to push on, no matter what I or any of the elders say. No matter how much we try to convince you it's a fool's errand."

Taunauk replied, "You're talking about defeating the Wolf King."

The elder mage nodded. "The Wolf King still lives. I'm sure there have been others too, in centuries past. Other groups of Chosen that sought escape. It's a cruel joke, if you ask me."

Helesys said, "You know you won't dissuade us."

"I know. Chetan tells us you seek passage through the seam? That can be arranged. However, there are protocols. You must prove yourselves worthy."

Shawn leaned against the back of the nearest metal chair. "How do we do that?"

Zinric's eyes widened with excitement. "The fighting pit, of course. How else would you display your prowess?"

Shawn guffawed. "How else!"

Helesys smirked, but Taunauk asked plainly, "How long does the proving last?"

"The meager sun will soon set, and we'll organize the fights tomorrow. Sleep well and you'll be on your way before tomorrow's end."

Helesys looked to her comrades, who nodded in turn. She replied, "That is satisfactory."

"Very well," Zinric replied. "I'll have Japag escort you to a suitable room." He pointed to the metal chair. "Don't worry. We'll give you padding."

~

As the three mages moved to leave, Helesys asked, "Elder, if you have a moment, I have questions about the elves."

Zinric paused for a moment, then waved the other mages in white away.

Neither Taunauk nor Shawn moved to leave.

Shawn shrugged against the metal chair. "I'm curious, myself."

Taunauk merely grunted, then sat cross-legged on the floor by the wall.

Helesys thought of her exchange with commander Chetan. "I do not remember much about my life outside the realms, but I remember the elven city of Novissimé. It was carved into the mountains, and it was the only elven city. Chetan had never heard of the city… Do you know of it?"

The elder mage brought a hand to his chin and considered this. He turned and peered out over the city for a long moment before turning back, a mixed expression on his face.

"I've never heard of that city. I remember some of the history, though now I fear it might be *ancient* history. Elves were the first Terrans—humans, the second. We were already making mithral when humankind discovered fire. For millennia, we lived separately. We strove not to interfere in the lives of men—this was our decree. But, alas, it did not stay that way.

"Ask yourself this, wanderers: What is better, to live long lives or to live short ones? Dwell on that, for that is the question between elves and humans. Our heroes, our inventors, our leaders live for centuries—some for millennia. Humans are flickers by comparison. Yet, the histories say that in only a single millennia the humans caught up to us. They learned to farm, to smelt iron, make steel, and harness magic.

"The others did not want to hear it, but I knew the truth. It was because of their short lives, their faster reproduction. What is one genius who lives a thousand years compared to one hundred geniuses? Even if they live shorter lives, their work compounds off one another, fresh eyes and fresh minds pushing ahead with youth and vigor.

"The humans were a young and hungry race, and I remember the whispers. In my youth, the elders were already afraid of being surpassed. There was talk of making a bastion in case the humans ever threatened our kind… But I never saw them start work on it. This city of Novissimé you speak of must be it."

As the elder spoke, his voice had grown weary. He continued, "So much time has passed… Sometimes I forget that the two worlds are not in parallel. Time moves much differently in here."

Helesys tried to fathom this. She thought of the memories of her mother and her sister, of the city and the Eternal War. "Does time move faster or slower in here than in the real world?"

Zinric shook his head. "I truly do not know. I've compared stories from other refugees, and I've thought it moved both faster and slower."

Shawn asked, "How can that be possible?"

The mage smirked. "You impose reason on an impossible place. Who are we to say what she decides?"

Silence fell over the room.

Shawn broke it. "She?"

But Helesys already knew. "The Gatekeeper."

Zinric nodded solemnly.

Shawn shook his head. "I'm sorry. I must've missed that part. Who is the Gatekeeper?"

Helesys replied, "We came across ruins in the Wode, and a green knight who spoke of her. She was a ruler of some kind, but the Wolf Knight took her as a queen, and then he became the king."

The elder mage nodded. "The Gatekeeper—the Queen— is the rightful ruler of the realms, but the Wolf King has usurped her.

Helesys's mind flashed back to Amadeus's tower, to the many questions they had asked—to the last question Helesys had asked before the Wolf King possessed the wizard's body and flung them to their deaths: *What of the Gatekeeper?*

Helesys tried to keep the trepidation from her voice as she asked, "Is it alright to speak of her? The Wolf King listens across the realms—"

Zinric held up a hand to stay her. "Our city is warded and ancient. The spires protect us."

Helesys and the others shared a glance. Amadeus's tower had been warded as well.

A moment later, Shawn said quietly, "What if the Voice at Meridian is the Gatekeeper? What if she's the one that's been helping us all along?"

Zinric rubbed his chin. "You wouldn't be the first to think that. I cannot imagine any other being able to overpower the Wolf King. It has to be her."

Silence fell again, and her comrades looked to Helesys.

"What is it?" Shawn asked, clearly seeing the worry on her face.

Helesys shook her head. "The Voice spoke to others. Even with the Voice's help and with the power of the Chosen, the others failed. *The Wolf King still lives*," she said solemnly, repeating what other creatures had echoed throughout the realms. "It doesn't matter," she decided. "Our path is set."

Zinric nodded. "Get some sleep. You have many lives ahead of you."

~

The heroes were led down the spiral stairs to another room big enough for five metal beds. Mattresses and pillows were laid out on three of them, each stuffed with dried straw and mosses. Two were left bare. A pile of blankets sat on another. Through the window, the red sky gave way to night and warm breeze to cool stillness.

Helesys sat on the edge of one bed, a sudden tiredness overtaking her. Shawn sat on another. Only Taunauk remained standing, staring at his bed.

"Is everything alright, big guy?" Shawn asked.

He glanced out the window and across the city, then sat his weapons and pack on the floor beside him.

When he finally sat on the bed, he sighed, and said, "I am going to stay awake a while, and talk to my father."

Shawn and Helesys eyed each other, both hesitant.

After a moment, Helesys asked, "What have you talked about?"

Taunauk's face remained set but his shoulders slumped at this, as if trying to maintain his composure was taking a physical toll on him.

"We speak of home, of the Endroggen plains where the green fields stretch farther than the endless sea. When we commune, it feels as if we're standing on those fields, though I do not see my home or any other Endroggen. We speak of training, and I have told him about our journey through the realms of this prison. Of our strength and hardships.

"But mostly we do not speak. When we do, the words come like intermittent rain. There is a divide between us, just as there always has been. I cannot be both a son and the vessel of my people. I know this. My father knows this. So we do not speak of much. It pains both of us—I can see it on his face—but we do not speak of this either. I have so many questions…"

Taunauk's face quivered at the end, and he fell silent. To see him stand against such fierce horrors across the realms, and to see him shaken now pained Helesys.

She said quietly, "You can speak with us, if it would help."

The barbarian shook his head. "I will use it. In time, pain smolders into memory, into rage. It is this way with all things." He met Helesys's eyes, the weariness giving ways to resolve. "That is your second lesson. In time, all things become rage. Your mother and your sister, one day they will only be memories, only rage, and you will have to carry that the rest of your life."

Helesys nodded, but Taunauk had already looked away. His skin and furs began to glow with soft golden light. He had already left to commune with his father.

Beside her, Shawn shook his head and wiped a tear from his eye. "It's not right. What kind of man won't talk to his son?"

Taunauk grumbled, "It is the way of things."

Shawn startled. "I didn't think you could still hear me."

"I can."

Shawn snorted. "*Stercus.*"

Helesys turned to the rogue. "What of you? Do you remember anything more about your life as a wisp? Or the man and the girl you lived with as a mortal?"

Shawn lay back and slumped against the wall next to his bed. "Being a wisp is… Well, it's hard to describe, really. It's like being drunk. One minute you're there, the next you're *there*. I can cross the realms and see people's thoughts—at least, some thoughts.

"As for my mortal life, that's just hazy. I didn't know the old man or his granddaughter—I'm sure of that. I think when I stopped being a wisp and became a Terran it was much like waking up here: No memories, no sense of purpose, no idea who I was. I think the old man and the girl took pity on me. Took me in. I miss them," he added, with a chuckle.

Shawn continued, "The strangest thing was, that for as beautiful and freeing as being a wisp was, when I put my wrappings back on and became corporeal, Terran, or whatever, it was even more beautiful. The sun and the wind felt so *real*. But I still don't get it."

Helesys asked, "What don't you understand?"

"I left my life as a wisp and became mortal. Then why did I come here? Why did I come here with you guys? For that matter, how did I go from factory worker to assassin, or whatever I am now?"

Helesys looked to their glowing comrade. "Perhaps we were meant to accompany Taunauk. Saving his people is a noble task."

Shawn nodded. "Okay, I'll buy that. That makes sense for you. You were elven royalty and a soldier. I was a factory worker... Okay, and I might've been an assassin." Shawn slumped all the way down onto his bed and stared at the ceiling. "Would it kill this place to let us have our memories?"

Helesys chuckled and laid down on her own bed. "We're not going to figure out any of it here, not tonight."

The weaver's mind drifted back to what Shawn said of his meeting with the voice. As she dwelled on the words, her frustration grew. "It doesn't seem right."

"What doesn't?"

"That it has to be you that kills the Wolf King."

Shawn shrugged. "Honestly, it's the least strange thing I've heard since we've been here."

Helesys shook her head. "What if we had never met?"

"I'm not following."

"Taunauk and I have been Chosen since we've been imprisoned here. What if we had never crossed paths with you? If we're mortal, and have no chance of defeating the Wolf King, then why give us the power in the first place?"

Shawn idly rubbed the wrappings around his forearms while he considered this. "We were always meant to find each other. We keep reuniting, even when we're separated."

"So what if you succumb to a lingering death? What then?"

Shawn shrugged again. "I know as much as you do."

Helesys scoffed. "I know. It's just... It just doesn't make sense. I can't explain it. What if the Voice is lying to us?"

Shawn smirked. "I had that thought too. But what else can we do, right?"

Helesys nodded reluctantly. "We might as well get some rest."

Shawn didn't reply. A moment later, she heard quiet snoring from his direction.

~

As she lay down, Helesys turned her attention inward to her wand and asked, *Are you still with me?*

*I am with you always, Helesys.*

*Can you tell me anything else about this place?*

*What the elder mage said was true about this place. Old magic runs deep within the city and the spires—magic that does not match the realm. Long ago, this city was forcibly brought from another realm. The spire bears the scars of that passage. Once, these furnishings were separate from the metal of the spire. Now they are melted together by the violent magics that brought it across the realms.*

Helesys considered this and could not disagree with her wand. Magic left scars on flesh, and she had seen the scars magic had left upon the Godpeak and the surrounding hills.

A question came to her unbidden. She asked, *Can we trust Zinric and the cabal?*

*It seems so. He is not hiding his intentions with magic and hasn't displayed any obvious tells that he is lying.*

Helesys rolled the image of the city over in her mind—the streets filled with vendors, the plentiful food. Overall, the people had seemed happy—something foreign to the dungeon.

She said, *It troubles me that we have seen few signs of civilization since we've been trapped. The village in the Wode was ruled by the Deacon, and the people did not seem as happy as this. The village beside the God-peak was nowhere near this size. There must be something…*

*…Something wrong,* her wand finished.

Yes.

*Consider this, Helesys Byyra: That not all wander as you do and seek escape. Some merely seek solace.*

*I've had this conversation before,* she replied. *It is not the people that trouble me. It's this place.*

*Let us hope that your worries are only specters.*

Helesys sighed quietly. *Do you remember what you were like before we were joined?*

*It is hard to say. Time passed differently then, just as it passes differently inside the dungeon than in the outside world.*

*Before you had someone to talk to all of the time?*

*Yes…* her wand answered reluctantly.

*Do you think time passed faster or slower?*

*I do not think time passed at all, Helesys.*

*What do you mean? Time is always passing. One moment is not the same as the one before or the one after.*

*Before we were joined, I had no reason to speak, to think, or to feel. I merely was. Does a castle consider each day when it cannot feel the sun rise or its people quiet and sleeping at night? How does a day pass to a tree? It may feel the sun but it doesn't have eyes to see or ears to hear the creatures that shelter beneath it. Perhaps each day passes in a blink.*

Helesys smiled in the dim room. *Now you're speaking in conjecture and philosophy.*

Her wand continued, *Consider a dreamless sleep. You do not speak or move or think, and a night seems to pass in an instant. I suspect before you, my existence was no different.*

The weaver paused to consider this, then shook her head. *You said that you were different—even from the Gar of Shéslang. Before me, you must have been bound to another.*

*Perhaps. If I was bound to another, I do not yet remember. You should sleep, Helesys. Who knows what tomorrow will bring.*

Helesys felt the voice of her wand drift away, like a receding tide pulling at her legs.

With any luck, her worries about Civirrea were misplaced, and the trials of tomorrow would be easy. She pushed these thoughts from her mind, let her wand's presence go, and welcomed sleep.

Dreamless sleep.


~  ~ ~

# A Test of Faith

The heroes were woken in the morning by footsteps outside their room. The servants brought bowls of steaming rice and vegetables, then waited patiently in the hall. Helesys and Taunauk sat on the floor to eat, while Shawn laid back on his bed. The barbarian ate quickly.

Shawn picked idly at his bowl. "What do you think they've got planned for us today?"

"Combat," Helesys replied absently.

"Well, yeah, I gathered that much from the fighting pit. I mean, what do you think we'll have to fight? I'm thinking it will be a dragon."

Helesys shook her head. "We already fought a dragon. Besides, I think they meant we would be fighting other warriors."

"They never said that."

Taunauk sighed and set the already empty bowl down. "I think it will be a monster. Something cunning."

The certainty with which he said it made the other two pause. Helesys asked, "What makes you say that?"

"They know we are not ordinary wanderers, that we are Chosen. They will not give us an ordinary beast—no matter how powerful. It would be too easy to overcome."

Shawn said, "You think they mean to kill us?"

"No," the barbarian replied. "But there is ritual at play here. They mean to challenge us and prove that we are worthy. I suspect the Chosen are held in high regard by the people here."

Shawn sighed. "I hate it when he's right. What about not giving breath to fate, huh?"

Helesys gestured with her spoon. "You were the one that started it." Taunauk shared a smirk. Shawn groaned and resumed eating.

Some minutes later, the elder mage entered the room. He wore the same long white robes as the previous day, but wore several thick and braided necklaces overtop it. His eyes, too, were ringed with markings.

"I trust the Chosen are rested and ready to begin?"

Shawn paused, mouth half-full. "What about time for our food to settle?"

Zinric chuckled. "It is a long walk to the pit, and there is still the ceremony to conduct. You'll have time."

Shawn shoveled another bite into his mouth, and the heroes rose to follow the elder mage.

~

They walked down the spire's central staircase and out onto the streets of Civirrea. Compared to the previous day, the streets were empty, and those that wandered stopped to watch the heroes with a mix of reverence and apprehension.

The fighting pit was situated in the heart of the city, ringed by spires. A dozen rows of seats filled with people ringed the single arena. The pit itself was not a colosseum like Helesys had imagined, but ruins of an ancient building—its floor was a mix of metal hills and valleys of hard-packed sand. All throughout were collapsed walls and towers, and a handful of still standing columns, all reminiscent of the melted metal furniture from the spires. The perimeter was warped and only vaguely circular, with three huge gashes in the metal wall that cut clean through and divided the crowd. Above each of the gashes was a small tower with raised seating—there sat a mixture of other mages and officials, each wearing vibrant robes. The red sky hung ominously above everything else.

At first, Helesys was weary of the open seats, as there seemed nothing that would protect the audience from an errant blast. She opened her senses to magic and found not only arcane barriers, but the subtle touch of the mages from the grandstands. Helesys had no way of knowing just how much protection the citizens would have, but she breathed easier knowing she wouldn't have to worry so much about her blasts.

The Zinric and the heroes stood between the spires, back far enough that the crowd hadn't seen them approach yet.

In those moments of calm, Helesys asked, "What happened here?"

"This was the sight of the Conflagration, where the Anaemon conducted the sorcery that stole this place."

Shawn muttered, "Why make it a fighting arena?"

The elder mage gave him a sidelong glance. "Many souls perished on that day. The Primattum objected and tried to stop the Conflagration. We prevailed. We honor their memories here."

"Oh," Shawn muttered. "They did this to themselves…"

Zinric turned, his brow set and voice measured. "The Anaemon had their reasons for doing what they did. They gave their lives for this purpose—for something greater than themselves."

Shawn turned away, clearly dwelling on what the elder said. He caught Helesys's eyes, a flicker of shame passing over his face before he turned away completely.

Helesys's gaze fell to the crowd and the twisted metal arena. Energy hung in the air, but the turmoil of her comrade overshadowed it.

Beside them, Taunauk stood stoically, his skin seeming to smolder with gold. "Let's get on with this. I grow weary of this realm."

"So be it," Zinric said. He stepped forward, his voice booming—amplified with magic. "Gathered citizens of Civirrea, we call you forth today to bear witness. These three are Chosen, and as they walk through our realm, they have agreed to heed our customs. To continue their journey, they must survive a trial by combat, and they must do so on our most hallowed ground—the ruins of Primattum and the birthplace of Civirrea!"

A thunderous applause echoed through the arena, and the elder mage turned to the heroes. "Take your place in the arena."

Taunauk led them down the central stairs, past the rows of citizens. Most cheered. Others shouted curses; most of these rang hollow to Helesys, but not all...

*Mendaxes*—liars.

*Psuedoprophetas*—false prophets.

She nearly turned to one such heckler, an elven man that spewed rice along with his curses, but Helesys stopped short.

He continued spewing insults despite her glare. She continued down the stairs.

And then another insult came: *The Wolf King still lives.*

Helesys grit her teeth and felt a quiet rage building within her. So what if there had been other Chosen that failed to kill him? Helesys was a soldier and a powerful sorceress. Taunauk was a vessel of his people, embodying dozens of spirits and eventually thousands. Shawn was already a god.

They would defeat the Wolf King. They would succeed where others had failed.

They had to.

~

The heroes took their places near the center of the arena, near one of the still standing columns. The metal beneath them seemed to smolder with magic, causing a shimmering haze to blanket the arena.

Helesys, Taunauk, and Shawn stood with weapons ready and power kindled.

Zinric's voice boomed over the arena. "First, our ancestors learned to survive in the barren desert realm of our once-home Primattum. Even in that inhospitable place, life found a foothold—We found a foothold. We learned to survive against the fearsome predators of the sand—*Moonwyrms.*"

The mages in the high seats stood and began to gesture in unison.

Beside her, Shawn whispered, "*Moonwyrms.* Sounds old. Know what it means?"

Helesys and Taunauk were already scanning the arena, and it was a moment before she replied, "It means *Moon Wyrms.*"

"What in Movernus's name is a…"

Shawn trailed off as magic swirled across the arena and co-alesced on the other side of the ruins. From the swirling purple, black, and red, came a cloud of sand. A quiet rustle of wind accompanied it as more and more grains fell from the cloud to the arena.

Inside, a long slender body writhed, and bat-like wingtips broke the surface of the cloud before disappearing again—a many-winged serpent. And it seemed to be growing larger. The cloud was some five feet cubed, then it was ten, then twenty. In moments, it grew until it was nearly a quarter of the arena. The cheers of the crowd grew with the creature.

From beneath the swirling cloud of sand emerged a square snout with viciously curved teeth. Its head was only vaguely reptilian—the scales closer to that of a fish than a lizard. It had no eyes that Helesys could see, and she could feel a magical presence about it, as if the creature was partly made of magic and ether.

She thought back to the Rithdai aboard the Idnauthi ship, and the foul magics that had made it. She felt—she knew—this was similar, but the only thing that escaped her lips was, "It is magical! Be ready!"

Meanwhile, Taunauk stepped forward and beat axe against his shield, goading the creature. "Come on!" Helesys and Shawn backed away, ready to flank the creature.

The serpent writhed low to the ground, its wingtips flashing to limbs as it half flew, half crawled across the arena. Then it lunged for Taunauk.

The barbarian crouched low, Everfall between him and the creature. In spite of his rage, he was nearly overshadowed by the maw of the giant creature. Helesys churned power and readied herself with bated breath for impact, to strike after Taunauk did.

But instead of the *Moonwyrm* slamming into Taunauk, Helesys felt a crackling of energy—

And another cloud of sand appeared right in front of Helesys, followed by the wyrm's gaping maw and jagged teeth.

Helesys's eyes went wide, and she leapt to the right, at the same time swinging the Gar of Shéslang. The tip slashed against the flank of the beast, drawing bright green blood. A shrill cry followed—

Another cloud to her left, the creature reappearing and lunging for her again. Helesys rolled away, keeping the spear between them and lashing out with a spreadblast from her gauntlet. Purple light flared, and the creature disappeared in a cloud of sand.

The arena around her glowed golden as a dozen Endroggen spirits surrounded her from all sides. Taunauk leapt across the hill and landed beside the group. This time, when the serpent appeared, it was met with flashes of blades, no matter which side. Four times it burst into sand and reappeared somewhere else, striving to attack a weak side of the group and finding none. Each time, the serpent's face and flank bled more green.

In the frenzy, Helesys searched for Shawn but couldn't see him anywhere. Instead, Helesys bolstered her power and felt the familiar rattle of her metal arm. She readied another spreadblast and crouched low, sure to keep the spear braced against the ground.

In the clouds of sand came another color, violent bursts of white and silver knives—and a rogue's familiar cackle, mixed with the increasingly frenzied cry of the serpent.

Then it came—a cloud of sand above her, followed by a great maw of teeth. Helesys raised her arm and fired as the beast was nearly close enough to touch. A great tearing sound echoed through the city, followed by a wet thump as the body of the Moon Wyrm landed a few paces away. Lifeless.

Helesys stood, covered in a spray of green blood. Beside her, Taunauk and the spirits relaxed their weapons. Shawn materialized a moment later.

"I love that trick," the rogue muttered as he adjusted his wrist wrappings. He sighed. "It's better than getting covered in gore."

Helesys smirked and wiped the blood from her face. It smelled like wet dirt. "Just don't go flying off again. Something tells me we're not done yet."

Shawn frowned. "*Stercus.* I can't do that trick a bunch or I just might."

Meanwhile, the cheers of the crowd swelled again, and Helesys knew that she was right.

Zinric's voice boomed across the arena. "Our ancestors learned how to forge metal with magic, how to build towering monuments and buildings that scraped the heavens. They made metal creatures, molded them for hard labor and to protect their great city. They took the power of the *Moonwyrms* and used it for their own."

The mages in the grandstands cast a spell in unison again. The arena began to rumble so violently that Helesys feared the very metal beneath her feet would split open.

Across the arena, a mountain of metal rose some fifteen feet high. It had the vague shape of a Terran—shoulders nearly as wide as it was tall, a small lump for a head—but the rest of it was a congealed mass of metal with only a hint of legs or arms.

Though it had no eyes, it looked at Helesys. Stared at her. The weaver churned power in response. Her muscles swelled and her arm hummed, the weaver thinking herself ready for anything.

Taunauk stood defiantly, weapons raised. Shawn cinched the black wrappings taut around his wrists and fumbled in his ethereal pouch for different daggers.

The metal began to whine as if it were being pressed and about to break. It grew until the steel beneath their feet and the arena all around was shrieking.

All around her, the Endroggen spirits clasped their ears and faded like snuffed candles. Helesys winced and churned power to weather the pain. She felt warm blood trickle down her neck—

Even with power, Helesys could bear it no longer. She raised her gauntlet and let loose a torrent of deadly purple. Some flew wild, shearing chunks of the landscape off, pieces scattering.

The metal man twisted its shoulders to dodge the blasts— such sudden movements that the creature didn't seem as if it had moved at all. As if it moved in the span of a blink.

The horrid whine of metal faded for just a moment, just enough time for Helesys to breathe, before it started again—

In another blink, the metal man crossed the arena and stood between the three heroes. Helesys and Shawn leapt back.

Taunauk roared and slashed with his axe, and again the creature slipped the blow. Taunauk lashed out with Everfall and the wooden shield struck true—the monster's whine cut short and was replaced with a deafening clang of impact.

The metal man reeled back before reaching three long arms out, one toward each of the heroes. Shawn slipped farther out of reach, Taunauk batted away the arm with his shield, and Helesys struck with the Gar of Shéslang. But when her spear collided with the arm, it flexed and seemed to melt around the spear.

The arena whined again, and the creature slid forward in a breath, seemingly to pull itself using Helesys's spear. It was in front of her, spear embedded in its body, its face blank as an uncarved doll. Helesys pulled once, but the spear didn't move.

The metal man reached toward her again, this time its spindly limb moving toward her gauntlet.

Helesys pulled again, and when she couldn't free the spear, she compounded her might with the Gar of Shéslang.

"*Restu sonmova, metala persa!*"

~

Helesys uttered the holding spell and felt the world give way to the shared mindspace between her and the metal man.

The sand of the arena and the few sandstone buildings surrounding it fell away, leaving only metal and darkness. The arena seemed to shrink before her eyes while the spires grew and grew until they disappeared somewhere in the swirling darkness of the sky. Soon, the spires had grown so tall and wide there was no space between them nor sky above. Meanwhile, the arena was no wider than the endless halls she had walked so very many times. It looked and felt as if she were encased in a bottle of metal.

As she looked around, the metal man appeared before her. It no longer towered over her—Helesys stood nearly a foot taller than it now—but it still stared with the same featureless expression.

To her surprise, Helesys saw another standing behind the creature—herself.

For a moment, Helesys's eyes flitted between the metal man and the copy of herself, unsure of what she was seeing or if both meant her harm. The metal man didn't move, and the copy seemed to mime her movements.

"Who are you?" Helesys asked.

"*I'm your wand,*" the copy replied. Everything about her seemed to copy Helesys's movements, except for her lips.

Helesys was taken aback by this. Speaking with her wand was such an intimate act, and the woman in front of her felt impossibly distant. It was a moment before she could speak— before she could push aside the discomfort.

Helesys breathed, then asked the metal man, and "What are you?"

"*You know what it is,*" mirror Helesys replied. "*It is a made-thing.*"

Helesys stared at the metal man, and found that it grew even smaller—to the stature of a child. It remained still, looking up at her.

"I should feel something, shouldn't I? Normally, I feel fear or power when I use the holding spell, but—" Helesys felt a pang of sadness in her gut. "What's wrong with it?"

"*It is a made-thing,*" her mirror repeated.

"There is nothing wrong with that—"

"*It isn't a matter of right or wrong, Helesys Byyra. A made-thing isn't whole, not like a human or an elf or even some of the monsters you've slewn. It is similar to a weapon imbued with magic, or a coin that leads the bearer to drink.*" At that, the mirror smiled.

"I shouldn't be able to hold it," Helesys muttered. "That's why it's staring at me. A Terran shouldn't be able to hold a made-thing." Helesys's mind flitted back to the dancer in Amadeus's tower and to Dissimul in One-Mind's lair.

"It's because of you, isn't it?" Helesys said to her mirror—to her wand. "You're why I can do those things. Why I can do so much more than other mages—why I can cast and conjure so many more different spells. It's our connection—our *direct* connection."

*"Yes. We are powerful together…"* There was a flicker of emotion on the mirror's face—of what, Helesys could not tell, for the moment was over.

The metal man crumpled. The mirror of Helesys vanished.

~

The shared mindspace of the holding spell disappeared, and Helesys was back in the arena of Civirrea.

The voice of Zinric boomed, "They are worthy!"

Taunauk and Shawn were beside her, both breathing heavily. The metal man lay in three pieces at her feet. As she looked down at it, she felt the same pang of sadness and confusion from earlier.

The metal man dissolved back into the metal of the arena, and the roar of the crowd drowned out everything else—

Except Helesys's questions.

~ ~ ~

# No Solace for the Chosen

The heroes were escorted from the arena by soldiers and the elder mage. As they climbed the stairs, the crowd cheered and some reached out for them. Helesys was vaguely aware of the errant hand on her shoulder or on her gauntlet, but she paid them no attention. Even as other warriors passed them on the stairs, making their own way down to the arena, Helesys spared them only a fleeting glance.

Two more elder mages, wearing the same white robes as Zinric, walked hastily up to their group. The first, a portly human with a scarred face and short hair leaned in close to Zinric's ear.

"They were not supposed to win," he seethed, speaking far too loudly to hide his words. "What are you going to do about this?"

Zinric leaned back and smiled patronizingly. "I'll forgive your tone, Tulver. You're young, and you forget the way of things. I'm going to do exactly as I our laws decree and exactly as the champions asked. I'm going to bring them before the Angel."

"You can't—"

"I will." Zinric walked on, waving for the heroes to follow. They did.

Helesys spared a glance to the new mages and to those in the grandstands. Though the people of Civirrea were cheering, none of their leaders reflected their mirth.

The angry mage met Helesys's eyes. "You're fools. The Wolf King still lives!"

Helesys had relinquished most of her power, but not all. She kept a quiet kindling of strength, should she need it.

She walked past the angry mages, leading Taunauk and Shawn out of the arena, and following Zinric through the city.

It wasn't until they'd turned the second corner through the streets that Helesys realized the commotion that was growing behind them. Part of the crowd was following them, chanting, "Long live the Chosen!" By the time they made it back to the spire, it seemed as if the entire city followed them.

Guards appeared at the spire's entrance and barred the crowd from following them inside. The heroes followed Zinric up the spiral stairs.

Shawn called from the rear of the group, "So, are you going to tell us what all that was about?"

"Yes," Zinric replied. "Let us find respite above."

He led them up two dozen flights before turning at a landing for a single large room. It seemed three stories tall and seemed to wrap halfway around the spire. Chairs littered the room, all melted and seamless from the floor.

The elder mage walked to the equally large window overlooking the city and turned to address them. "This was once a room of government and decree. It's fitting that it should see something as monumental as the truly Chosen."

Taunauk grumbled, "Speak plainly." The barbarian stood so that he could see both the mage and the stairwell. Footsteps echoed up the stairs.

Zinric continued, "So many claim to be Chosen, but it is an easy thing to claim, isn't it? Harder to verify. What my compatriot, Tulver, said was true–you were not meant to survive. Only the truly Chosen can survive our trials."

Helesys scoffed. "Or just someone powerful. There was nothing in your *trial* that marked us as Chosen."

Zinric smirked. "I suppose, but the powerful don't wander the realms like you do. They find somewhere with relative peace, then stake their claim. Surely you've seen what I speak of–the masters of their own little realms. Only the naive and the Chosen wander like you."

Shawn said, "So then you kill them? What's the point?"

"To make sure they're ready. If they survive, then we bring them before the Angel for judgment."

Helesys shared a frustrated glance with Shawn, while Taunauk looked expectantly toward the stairs.

Helesys said, "I think we're done here. Whatever you and the other mages believe, we completed your ritual. Now take us to the seam."

She was already kindling power, the metal of her right hand humming with violent anticipation–a reflex.

Zinric glanced at her gauntlet apprehensively and then looked her in the eye. "I know you're powerful, and I would likely pose you no threat–let alone all three of you. But the rest of the cabal is on its way here and would have no qualms about killing you outright. Could you fight twenty mages? What about an angry mob? Would you–"

"Get to the point," Helesys growled.

"You want the seam. It lies beneath the city, where the Angel dwells. As I said, you are going before the Angel for judgment. It *may* let you pass."

Silence fell, and Helesys was vaguely aware of the audience huddled on the stairwell. Several mages and guards peered in. Taunauk stood at the door, axe in hand.

"Fine," Helesys said. At that, Taunauk relaxed, and others filed in. Helesys added to Zinric, "We'll meet your the Angel. I'm tired of waiting."

The portly Tulver pushed past and stood between Helesys and Zinric. "See," he said, pointing to her gauntlet, "that's what you get when you consort with Chosen." His face wrinkled in disgust at Helesys, "Now, stand down."

Helesys grit her teeth and forced herself to relax her gauntlet–but she kept her kindled power. If she would submit to meeting the Angel, then she would give no more concession.

"It's fine," Zinric said, patting the angry mage on the shoulder. "They're going to meet the Angel now. In an hour you can go back to the arena and then rest easy tonight."

A hint of a smile flashed across Tulver's face and was gone in a moment. "Very well, Zinric. Get on with it."

Zinric walked to the door and beckoned them to follow him down the stairs. Helesys shared glances with her comrades, each mirroring her apprehension. She walked with kindled menace past the gathered mages and guards, toward the bottom of the spire.

~

They descended the metal stairs and passed through the melted barroom at the bottom. Zinric led them to a small back room, where he muttered words to quiet for Helesys to make out.

Another staircase appeared in the metal, and the elder led them ever deeper. Behind them, trailed a dozen more souls—a mix of guards and mages. Helesys didn't search their faces to see if Tulver was among them.

The stairwell grew dark, and the mages conjured light. Zinric held a small flame in his palm that cast flickering shadows on the walls. Helesys conjured her own warding light—still hesitant to trust their escorts.

Helesys focused on the odd twists and turns of the stairwell. Once again, she felt a lingering magic written into the place just as she had felt in the ruins at the bottom of the sea. Even the engravings were eerily similar—all runes of containment.

"We saw these same runes before," Helesys said. "These runes are made to trap power. Is your Angel not a willing ally?"

Zinric sighed. "Our arrangement is complicated. The Angel is not a Terran in the sense of elves and humans. The Angel is a celestial. Some believe them to be our predecessors from primordial times. Others think of them as demons or their antithesis. Others believe that they are from the stars or another dimension. I do not know."

The annoyed voice of Tulver sounded from the back of the group, "It's not your place, Zinric. You say too much."

"Silence, Tulver. They deserve to have their questions answered, to know the gravity of their situation… To know what they're about to see." Zinric trailed off, his voice hesitant.

Shawn said, "He isn't a sight for Tamir, is he? Be honest. We've seen some godsawful things in the realms."

Zinric spoke over the audible groan from the back of the group. "It is not a sight for *mortals*, my poor fellow. But you are Chosen... What do you have to fear?" They reached the bottom of the stairs as he finished, and Helesys found her dread mounting.

Something wasn't right with this arrangement–yet they had no choice. Whatever else Zinric might have been lying about, the seam was down there. Helesys could feel it.

She expected the halls to twist and branch out like they had in the ruins beneath the sea. Instead, Zinric led them down a single straight hall. As they walked, Helesys eyed the strange runes engraved on the metal... They were not the same un-readable script that had covered the walls of the ruins of Antrikaumora–

Her wand could translate these words:

*A choir of angels before the fall*
*plucked like mandolin strings*
*cut down like thrall.*
*An ensemble wandering in desert sun*
*bringing death and turmoil*
*till Enchiridion come.*
*Monarchs looming amidst metal spires*
*Angels take their places*
*all others retire.*
*No sooner shall they reign*
*then chattel revolt.*
*"Spare us", the masses cried*
*while angels lament their escape*
*the city boils and we sever our ties*
*For faith to live, nine must die*
*One must survive*

*All in favor, say I*
*Sing no more*
*Our work is done*
*—Wolf God our witness*
*—the never-risen sun*

"Move along, sorceress," Tulver hissed. "Don't pretend—"

Helesys held up her elven hand to silence him as she finished reading. "It's a chronicle... Was this written by the Angel?"

"Yes," Zinric said, pausing with flame in hand. "It's the story of the Angel bringing Civirrea across the realms. I've never met one that could read it." He hesitated for a moment, as if there was something else he wanted to say to Helesys, but instead turned up the stairs. "Do you believe now, Tulver?" He turned without waiting for a response.

As the end of the hall grew near, there were flickering shadows, as if someone were dancing in the firelight. The sound of wet, ragged breaths echoed from beyond.

It was in those last steps that the writing on the wall changed. Helesys's stomach turned, and she felt the hum of warning from her wand—all too late.

More words were scrawled in the same language as the runes—cut into the metal with deep gashes:

*THE CHOSEN ARE A LIE.*
*THE CHOSEN ARE A LIE.*
*THE CHOSEN ARE A LIE.*

The words wrapped around the walls, the ceiling, the floor, and still Zinric walked forward unperturbed, leading them into the firelit room.

Behind her, Shawn muttered, "What in Movernus's name…"

"Nothing good," Helesys replied, hoping that her comrades would heed her subtle warning.

They came to a sprawling circular room, a cylinder that rose some fifty feet overhead. All the surfaces were slick metal, polished to a glistening sheen. Great twisting columns rose from the floor and stretched haphazardly to the ceiling.

And across it all were great scorch marks, as if two blistering fingers had been raked angrily across swathes of the room.

Somewhere in the tangled grove of metal was the source of light and ragged breaths. As it flickered, the light seemed to travel up the columns like water clouding a pipe.

"Bring them here," the voice said, the words making Helesys shiver. She knew it was no Terran—no elf or human. The voice sounded pained, as if it was not meant to come from flesh.

Zinric led them closer to a clearing in the metal. There stood a glowing figure. Its shroud of light seemed the same hue as the metal and obscured most of its features. It stood nearly fifteen feet tall, its body slender and Terran in form. Though gaunt, its muscles and bones were pronounced. Its head was large and bulbous, most of its features hidden—save for its eyes, that were huge pools of light three times too large.

"Closer," it said.

The mages and soldiers stopped and urged the heroes forward. The three walked with trepidation.

It said, "It has been a long time since I have met the Chosen ones… Too long." There was a muttering behind them, and the creature hissed, "*Silence*. It is fate that you come before me, not chance, my chosen ones. Do you recognize this place?"

Helesys answered, "This place is like the ruins beneath the sea."

From behind the veil of light came a nod. "Good, weaver, except they are not ruins. That place was built for one thing and one thing only—to safeguard the Machine of Antrikaumora. I have seen it. I have walked those magic-laced stairs, my brethren and I.

"We descended the stairs in agony, for they and I were beings of magic. In the end, we could not take the Machine for ourselves.

"In our travels, we learned of the Wolf King—the god of this world, of all the realms. His word and his will became our own."

"We found Primattum and its towering metal spires—already ancient, its makers long forgotten. We supplanted its rulers, took it for our own. We ruled in his name. We thought we'd found a home, a kingdom to rule as was the old ways, but it was not meant to last. Our city revolted, and we were forced to flee.

"We pooled our might and stole this city. Our loyal inhabitants did not survive, nor did my brethren—all nine of them. Slowly, wanderers came to me, and in time, I rekindled this forgotten piece of metal in the barren sands.

"I hollowed out the metal beneath Civirrea, and made these depths in its image of Antrikaumora. A place to channel my own power and to call the bearer of the Machine. In your haste and ignorance, you answered. The Machine will not aid you. The Wolf King still lives. He is the Never-Risen Sun. His life is eternal.

"Do you have any last words, Chosen ones, before I smite thee in his name?"

Helesys's heart was in her throat, and her comrades had already taken fighting stances. She was vaguely aware of shuffling steps behind her as the mages and soldiers backed even farther away.

It was a long moment before the weaver found her voice. Her mouth was dry. "You are wrong. We've met creatures that have seen the sun rise."

"Blasphemy."

"Perhaps you're not as ancient as you think," she said quietly.

For a moment, the Angel seemed to consider this, but then its eyes–the pools of light–began to grow bright as lightning. Helesys didn't need the rattle of her wand-arm to know that such a thing meant death.

"*Lente et gravis!*" Helesys shouted.

Helesys, Taunauk, and Shawn were already leaping to the side when light flared in the room–two thick beams of light shot from the Angel's eyes and lanced across the room. A sound like thick glass vibrating rang out and grew painful. As Helesys landed on her side, she felt the intense heat behind her and instinctively rolled as far away as she could.

When she turned to look, two massive scorch lines had cut through the room. A soldier lay in three scorched pieces in the midst of it. The other mages and soldiers were already running down the hall in retreat.

Briefly, Helesys considered trying to hold the terrible creature, but knew intrinsically that she could not—it was far too powerful for such a spell.

The Angel was already turning. And as Helesys saw the creature from the side, she saw a completely different image.

Instead of a Terran behind the light, she saw a many-limbed abomination, a body like a tangled mass of spider web and gore—the true body of the creature.

Twin lances of light swept across the room. Helesys and Taunauk ducked under the beams, the heat feeling dangerously close. Taunauk lunged forward, slashing. There was a deep metallic hum as Taunauk's blade struck the golden creature again and again. Then light flared, and the barbarian was sent hurtling through half a dozen smoldering pillars of metal.

Helesys raised her gauntlet, churning what little power she could spare and let arcane blasts fly. In her desperation, only half struck true, sending the Angel staggering backward from the assault.

"Weaver, do you think your paltry magic will save you!"

The Angel turned toward her, and its light grew blinding. It was pushing back against her counter magic—trying to shake off her *slow* spell. Helesys pushed back, siphoning power from the Gar of Shéslang to bolster herself. For a moment, she held her own against the terrible creature.

Again came the whine of vibrating glass—

Beams of light burst across the room, this time winking in and out. The creature cried out, a deep roar that rattled the metal around them and the teeth in Helesys's skull. The beams flashed wildly across the room. In the haze of light, Helesys saw a dozen forms assailing the Angel—no doubt Taunauk and his spirits, and a blur that could've only been Shawn.

Shawn cried out, "Use the Machine!"

Helesys reached in her pocket for it, but as she touched the cold metal cube, her heart fell.

*It is not like other artifacts,* her wand said. *The Machine of Antrikaumora does not recharge itself. Its power is finite, and there may only be a few moments within it. If you use it now, you will lose all hope of defeating the Wolf King.*

Helesys groaned in frustration. Across the room, light flared again, striking one of the Endroggen spirits—

For a moment, the room went dark, and Helesys felt her stomach wrench. Even from afar, she felt utter anguish as the spirit was snuffed out. It was only a moment, and then light returned to the battlefield—that of the Angel and the spirits.

Taunauk's axe flashed wildly, and the hall filled with screams of creature and metal.

"Damn you, weaver!" the Angel howled.

Again, the silver light of the thing grew blinding, and Helesys felt it push back against her spell. She summoned the rest of the spear's power—still the Angel pushed, threatening to cast off her magic.

Helesys had already called on the full might of her wand and the spear, so she turned desperately inward. She could not fail—would not fail. Without her *slow* spell, the creature would lay waste to them. Without her, they would fall to a lingering death.

She thought of Taunauk and Shawn, of how far they had come, how much they had suffered and struggled already, and resolved that they would not fall—not here—and they would not fail.

She thought of the Angel, of its twisted form and terrible power—pushed these aside. Instead, she thought of its audacity—that it would *dare* stand in her way.

She thought of her mother and her sister, of memories stolen by the dungeon, of memories that she had yet to reclaim.

And so Helesys found an inner strength—the first tappings of Rage. The elf grew mighty, and in that moment, she stood against an ancient god and held her ground, while her comrades carved the life from it.

~

"Enough!" came a hoarse, inhuman cry.

The maelstrom of steel and power faded, leaving silence and the pained gasps of the Angel. The hall of twisted metal was nearly dark, lit only by the fading light of the creature. It lay in a heap in the clearing, its eldritch, many-limbed form no longer hidden by the light. It was more insect than Terran, and even now, neither Helesys nor her comrades could look at the strange form for more than a moment.

Helesys felt the Angel's strength fade and she knew that this was no bluff.

"I will let you go," it said. "I will no longer—can no longer fight you. I beg, do not make me wander again."

Taunauk snorted angrily, hands squeezing the wrappings of his axe. Meanwhile, Shawn's face was twisted into a sneer, his form ghostly.

Helesys stepped forward and put a hand on the barbarian's shoulder. "Its power is gone."

Taunauk shrugged his shoulder and pulled away from her. He let the axe fall to the floor. "I… I cannot feel her anymore. One of my people is lost forever. One of the souls I swore to protect, that I came here to protect, that I was raised…" Taunauk's fists were clenched and shaking.

The Endroggen glowed golden and at once his body relaxed. He stared across the room, quiet tears beading in his eyes.

Helesys turned and sighed—at least Taunauk hadn't lost his father to the creature.

Shawn was rewrapping his forearms. "You're lucky," he whispered to the Angel.

The creature whimpered. "You will never win. He is eternal."

"You are wrong," Helesys said. She knelt beside the creature so that there was no mistaking her words. "The sun has risen twice in the dungeon's past—twice, at least."

"The Wolf King still lives…"

Shawn said, "Maybe the other Chosen got close, but they didn't finish the job. *That's what the voice was trying to tell me…* The wrong hero landed the killing blow. That would explain it. So many realms we've wandered have been stuck in perpetual twilight. If the Wolf King was dead, shouldn't the sun *stay* risen?"

The Angel laughed, wet and hoarse. "Even the fool among you sees."

Realization dawned on Helesys. "They didn't have the Machine of Antrikaumora. We do." She stood with new resolve. "We'll see the sun rise on the realms."

Both Helesys and Shawn looked to Taunauk. The barbarian still faced away from them. He stooped for his axe, then stowed it in his backsling. "Let's go. I grow weary of this realm."

Helesys glanced once more at the fallen god, but when she found it still, she turned her attention to the seam. She reached out and grasped it, wrenched it open, and peered through the realms.

"Be quick," the Angel said. "*He* knows."

Helesys searched for the castle, for the topmost reaches where she thought the Wolf King would dwell. Clean stone, carpet, banners, and art.

"Come," she said. "Our destiny awaits."

~ ~ ~

NEXT TIME ON
*A BATTLEAXE AND
A METAL ARM*
Book 15:

*Gallery of Mourning*
Available June 2022

# Spoiler–Free excerpt from *BAMA 15*

The heroes pressed forward down the immaculate, and seemingly unending hall. They stalked in silence, for the deeper they went, the more certain the feeling of mounting dread. It etched in their minds like weather and rain did stone, boring through them, hollowing them.

Helesys kindled power, trying instead to fill herself with determination, but it felt like shoring a candle against a storm. She had seen the things that gods could do. She had seen wonders and horrors wrought across the realms—from across history and space—compressed into the madness that was the dungeon. She had seen more in her short journey across the realms that most others would ever dare to look upon. And she knew that the Wolf King towered above all these.

When one had walked among gods, and fought against gods… What words were there for something like the Wolf King? A singularity amongst the world.

Helesys resisted the urge to touch the tiny cube in her pocket, the Machine of Antrikaumora, that supposedly would allow them to stand equal to the God of gods—

To slay *him*.

In those quiet moments of the hall, it felt not just impossible, but absurd.

Yet, they walked forward, bore on by mix of will, desperation, promise of salvation, or destiny—it did not matter why. It only mattered that they walked forward.

To be continued June 2022

# Thank you for Reading

I hope you enjoyed reading this story as much as I enjoyed writing it.

If you did, I would massively appreciate a short review on Amazon or your favorite book website. Reviews are crucial for any author, and a starred review or even just a line or two can make a huge difference.

It's especially true for the start of a series. Thanks and I hope you enjoy the next one!

# Looking for more Engrossing Fantasy?

You might like ***Tales from Another World,*** an ongoing short story series containing stories about sorcerers, druids, mortals, gods, thieves, and all other manner of Terrans.

The $2^{nd}$ and $3^{rd}$ installments are out and they tie into the outside world of *A Battleaxe and a Metal Arm*. So, if you're looking for more engrossing fantasy stories, and if you want to know more about this fantasy universe, read on and see how deep the rabbit hole goes.

# What questions do you have about *A Battleaxe and a Metal Arm?*

If you've read this far, hopefully you'll read a bit further—both in this book and across the series. I'm not sure how most authors write serials and how much of it is flying by the seat of their pants, but that's not how I do things. For all the major questions that might come up in BAMA, I already have answers for 95% of them. Same goes for the major plot points, twists and climaxes. That might sound boring to some, especially some of you other authors who enjoy variations of writing into the dark, but I think having a solid blueprint is paramount to writing a long series.

So, what questions do you have about the story? Here are a few:

1) ~~What is the dungeon?~~ It's a soul trap of overwhelming size and power. But where did it come from? Is it a force of nature or an ill-made weapon, or perhaps something else entirely? In the real world, it looks like a giant cloud with faces writhing just beneath the surface. Helesys speculates that the

reason no one remembers it is because it's so horrific their minds blot it out!

2) ~~Who was Helesys before she got trapped~~? We've learned that Helesys was both a soldier and was the oldest daughter of the elven Great House Byyra.

3) ~~Who was Taunauk before he got trapped~~? There was an omen of a blight in the Endroggen heaven, Accaelum. Taunauk is an Endroggen barbarian who was raised as a warrior and a vessel. His purpose was to one day free the trapped Endroggen souls from the Dungeon.

4) How well did they know each other beforehand?

5) How did Helesys get her metal arm? Likely through injury, amputation, and replacement. She was likely fighting in the Eternal War, the war of the Elves against the Shadowkind.

6) ~~Who is Shawn~~? He is a wisp from the plane of dreams. One who walks through the dreams of elves and humans, while being neither. He has lived as both a god and a mortal.

7) Why does Shawn feel so familiar to Helesys and Taunauk? The group speculates that they were traveling together for unknown reasons. Shawn worries that they were tracking him. This could explain why Helesys and Taunauk are always reborn together, while Shawn was usually alone.

7) Who is the Wolf King and what sinister plans does he have for our heroes? How did he come to rule over the Dungeon? How does the Gatekeeper factor into all this?

8) Who is the mysterious voice encountered on the white sandy shores of Meridian? Why do they seek the death of the Wolf-King? …And why did they choose the heroes? The Voice might be the Gatekeeper… but the truth is still unknown…

Did I miss any questions? Probably. Connect with me and other *BAMA* fans on social media and compare questions!

I've got plans. I've got answers. And I've got them on a drip-feed. Keep reading and expect to find out a little more to the mysteries with each installment. Hopefully, you're as excited about this series as I am.

# Connect with the Author

If you want to stay up to date on the latest about Samuel's publishing news and blog, check out his website and consider signing up for his monthly newsletter.

www.SamuelFlemingBooks.com

Samuel can also be found on Reddit, Tiktok, and Facebook.

Samuel Fleming is a Science Fiction and Fantasy author.

He grew up in Maryland, spending most of his time swimming and writing. Swimming gave him a lot of time to daydream, so the two hobbies complemented each other well. Idle day dreams turned into stories, some of which stuck with him for years. These days he swims a little less and writes a lot more.

He loves a good story no matter the medium: Books, TV, video games, comics, tabletop RPG's, or podcasts—most of which he attempts to share with his wife and three kids, and occasionally on his blog.

www.ingramcontent.com/pod-product-compliance
Lightning Source LLC
Chambersburg PA
CBHW030649190726
48286CB00008B/2739